In the middle of a lovely garden
was a big house with fourteen rooms.
Danny D, Michael, Christy, David,
Mommy, and Daddy
lived there.

The garden had
lots of red flowers,
many more blue flowers,
and a very tall
pine tree on one side.

Danny D asked Papa Stu,
"Does the top of that tree touch heaven?
"No," said Papa Stu.
"And, Danny D, do you know that birds can
fly so high above that tree
that we can hardly see them?"

"Higher than the clouds, Papa Stu?
Will they fly right into heaven?"

Papa Stu stooped down
so he could see
right into Danny D's eyes.
"No, Danny D,
heaven is far away
and God is there.
But God is other places, too.
ALL AT THE SAME TIME!"

Danny D could
hardly believe that.

On the other side
of the garden
was a pretty pond.
Fourteen frogs played there
on the lily pads.
But when Danny D tried to catch one,
all of them swam down, down, down
to the bottom of the deep pond.
They swam down so far
that Danny D couldn't
reach them.

Papa Stu smiled.
He patted Danny D's head.
Then Papa Stu stooped down
so he could see
right into Danny D's eyes.
Papa Stu said,
"God is very clever.
God is everywhere.
He can go deeper
than the frogs can swim.
He can go higher than
the birds can fly.
In fact, he can be up
and down
at the same time!"

Danny D could
hardly believe that.

Mommy was in the kitchen
making chocolate chip cookies.
Daddy was in the den reading a book.
Christy was in the playroom with her toys.
Michael and David were in the basement playing with their trucks.
Papa Stu and Danny D were outside raking the lawn.

"Is God with us here?" Danny D asked.
Papa Stu smiled.
He patted Danny D's head.
Then Papa Stu stooped down so he could see right into Danny D's eyes.
Papa Stu said, "God is everywhere, Danny D. In fact, he is inside all the rooms in the house and outside with us at the same time!"
Danny D could hardly believe that.

Mommy and the other children went shopping.
Daddy went to work at his church.
Papa Stu and Danny D went fishing.
When they were out of the
house, no one was in;
everyone was out.
EXCEPT God was
IN AND OUT!

Even when God
goes out, he's in.
God was with
everyone at
the same time!

Danny D could
hardly believe
that.